P9-DDB-058

# The Hickory Chair

by LISA ROWE
FRAUSTINO

illustrated by
BENNY
ANDREWS

Arthur A. Levine Books
AN IMPRINT OF SCHOLASTIC PRESS

LIBRARY OF CONGRESS CATALOGING-IN-PUBLICATION DATA

Fraustino, Lisa Rowe.
The hickory chair / by Lisa Rowe Fraustino; with pictures
by Benny Andrews  p.  cm.
Summary: A blind boy tells of his warm relationship with
his grandmother and the gift she left him after her death.

ISBN 0-590-52248-5

[I. 2.] I. Andrews, Benny, illu. II. Title. PZ7.F8655BI
2000 [ E ]—dc21 99-019815

Text type is set in 17-point Goudy Modern MT.
Display type is set in Steam. • The artwork is done in
oils and fabric collage. • Book design by Marijka Kostiw

10 9 8 7 6 5 4 3 2 1          01 02 03 04 05

Printed in Mexico on acid-free paper    49
First Edition, February 2001

WE WOULD LIKE TO THANK OUR COLLEAGUES
AT THE NATIONAL BRAILLE PRESS FOR THEIR
HELP AND ADVICE ON THIS BOOK.

For Olivia, in memory of her godfather,
Louis D. Mitchell
— L. R. F.

To my grandson,
Casey Robert Andrews
— B. A.

Sundays when I was small, that Gran of mine was good at hiding. The first time I played hide-and-seek with her and the older grandchildren, she disguised me as the pillow on the bed that Gramps had carved long ago for my father. Nobody found me.

When I was the seeker, I could almost always sniff everyone out,

even Gran the time she stood inside her robe behind the bathroom

door. She had a good alive smell—lilacs, with a whiff of bleach.

I loved Gran's smell, and her warm face when we played touch-your-nose at the gold mirror, and her salty kisses when we sat on Gramps's old army trunk in the attic and listened to the wind sing on the roof.

Most of all, I loved her molasses voice as she read to me out loud.

"You're my favorite youngest grandchild, Louis, and this is my favorite chair," she'd tell me. "Gramps carved it from a hickory that once grew on this very spot." She clapped her hands together. Lilac and bleach danced around.

"Every time I sit in this chair, I lean back, shut my eyes, and see that old hickory tickling the belly of the sun."

"Me too," I said, and I really did see it, even though I was born blind.

"You got blind sight," said Gran, and she tickled my nose.

So the Sundays went until one day in school, I felt my father's shad-

ow cold on my cheek. He told me Gran had died.

At the funeral I touched her hand to say good-bye. It was cold and

smelled too much of lilacs, not enough of bleach.